Little
HORRORS

Shiver with fear...

Owww!

...shake with laughter!

For Philip Bleach

Visit Shoo Rayner's website!
www.shoo-rayner.co.uk

ORCHARD BOOKS
96 Leonard Street, London EC2A 4XD
Orchard Books Australia
32/45-51 Huntley Street, Alexandria, NSW 2015
First published in Great Britain in 2003
First paperback edition 2003
Copyright © Shoo Rayner 2003
The right of Shoo Rayner to be identified as the author
and illustrator of this work has been asserted by him in
accordance with the Copyright, Designs, and Patents Act, 1988.
A CIP catalogue record for this book is available
from the British Library.
ISBN 1 84362 006 5 (hardback)
ISBN 1 84362 010 3 (paperback)
1 3 5 7 9 10 8 6 4 2 (hardback)
3 5 7 9 10 8 6 4 2 (paperback)
Printed in Great Britain

Little HORRORS

The Bone Man

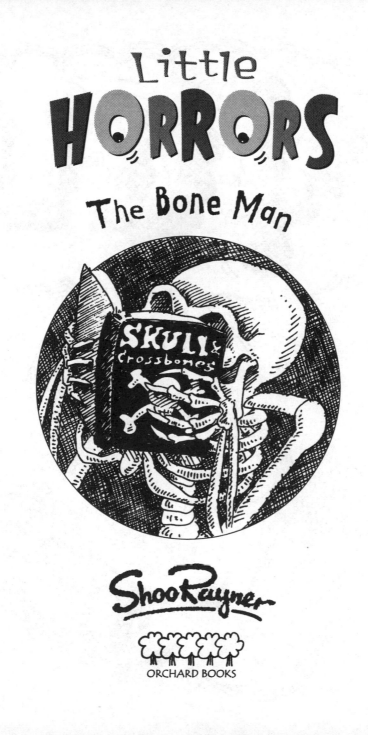

Shoo Rayner

ORCHARD BOOKS

It was horrible!

My sister, Kim, and I were staying
with Aunt Loopy.

Her dog, Treacle, had jumped into
the pond and shaken cold, slimy
water all over me!

"Come here, you little terror!"
I shouted, chasing Treacle out
of the back gate and into the
wilderness beyond.

Treacle ran and ran until I lost sight of her.

We waited ages for her to come back, but she had just vanished!

Aunt Loopy spoke in a creepy voice. "I hope Whistling Jack hasn't got her."

Shivers ran up and down my spine.

"Who's Whistling Jack?" I asked.

"He was a terrifying pirate who whistled tunes while he tortured his enemies," said Aunt Loopy.

"Stories say that he was buried with his treasure, somewhere here in the wilderness. His ghost whistles to frighten away treasure seekers."

As I looked for Treacle, I heard a weird, muffled barking from below my feet.

I bent down to listen and my stomach lurched.

The ground was swallowing my left leg!

"Yeeurgh!"
Something cold
and wet pressed
against my ankle!

"Yaaargh!"
Hot, clammy
breath rippled
over my leg.

"Hurrgh!"
Something bristly
licked my knee!

Panicking, I yanked my leg out.
A whistling sound drifted out of
the hole. My blood ran cold.

"It's Whistling Jack!" I shouted.
"I can hear him!"

Aunt Loopy ran over and peered into the hole. "It's Treacle!" she laughed. "She must have fallen down the hole like you did."

She grabbed Treacle's collar, and pulled her out.

Treacle bounced about, proudly
showing off the bone she held in
her mouth.

When she breathed, the bone
made a squeaky, tooting whistle!

Aunt Loopy examined the bone.

"How interesting," she said. "That's what was making the noise. We should show this to an expert."

The next day we went to the museum to see the museum's bone expert, Dr Spindleshanks.

You could hardly move in
Dr Spindleshank's office.

On a pile of books, a human
skeleton sat grinning at us!

We froze in horror! A dry, dusty voice said, "Hello," behind us, making us jump out of our skins!

An old man stood in the doorway. He was so bald and thin, he looked like the skeleton's brother!

"I'm Dr Spindleshanks," he croaked. "How can I help you?"

When Aunt Loopy had recovered from the fright, she showed him the piece of bone.

He checked it with the skeleton, and became very excited when we told him where we had found it.

We had to show him the exact spot on a map.

His eyes narrowed and he whispered to himself, "It could be where Whistling Jack is buried!"

He winked at us. "Keep this a secret. If word gets out, the place will be full of treasure seekers with metal detectors. We'll start investigating tomorrow."

That night, we were making hot chocolate in the kitchen. Kim looked really worried.

"What if it *is* where Whistling Jack is buried?" she asked. "He won't haunt us, will he?"

"T-t-t-there's no such thing as ghosts," I said, hopefully.

As I spoke, Aunt Loopy's cats, Itchy, Scratchy and Nits, tore through the cat-flap, hissing and spitting.

Treacle growled and pawed to be let out of the back door.

Through the window, far out in the dark wilderness, two glowing, red eyes swayed hypnotically.

Aunt Loopy opened the back door a crack. An eerie sound floated across the still night air...

...someone or something was...
WHISTLING!

Treacle barked and burst through the door.

I'm sure I saw something in the distance as Treacle went in for the attack.

It looked like a living skeleton!

"It's Whistling Jack!" I hissed.

There was a terrible wailing and whistling and barking, before the red eyes snapped off and all went quiet.

34

With a torch and a walking stick to protect us, we crept out into the darkness. Something was whistling in the hole!

Had Whistling Jack got our Treacle?

Aunt Loopy's torch lit up the ghastly scene.

Treacle stood guard over a pale, thin body. It raised a scrawny, bony hand.

It spoke with a thin, ghostly voice.

"Dr Spindleshanks!" we all cried.

Back in Aunt Loopy's house,
Dr Spindleshanks showed us his
metal detector.

It had two red lights on the front
and it whistled when it found
something. That's what we had seen
and heard.

He hung his head. "I'm sorry, I couldn't wait until tomorrow. I wanted to be the one who found Whistling Jack's treasure."

"So you think it really is where Whistling Jack is buried?" Aunt Loopy asked excitedly.

Dr Spindleshanks shook his head. "No, that hole is probably an old fox's lair. The bone you found came from a fox's dinner."

"If the story of Whistling Jack's treasure is true," he continued, "I think someone would have found it by now."

Phew! We went to bed happy. There was no ghost of Whistling Jack after all.

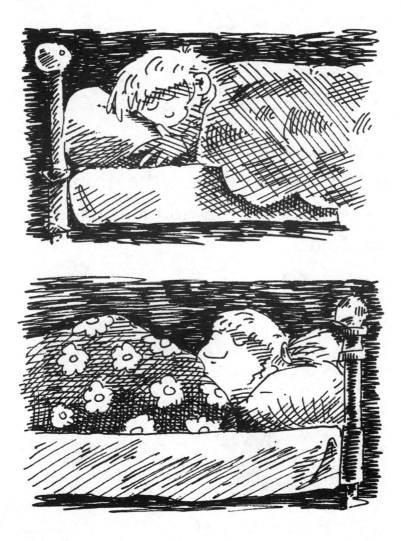

The next day we went for another walk and Treacle disappeared again.

Weird, warbling whistles drifted out of another hole in the ground. I stuck my arm in and felt around for Treacle.

Something wet
and bristly licked
my other hand.

Something wet
and bristly also
licked my face.

It was Treacle!

If she wasn't in the hole, then who
or what was?

And who or what was whistling that creepy, eerie tune?

Little Horrors by Shoo Rayner

❏ The Swamp Man   1 84121 646 1
❏ The Pumpkin Man   1 84121 644 5
❏ The Spider Man   1 84121 648 8
❏ The Sand Man   1 84121 650 X
❏ The Snow Man   1 84362 009 X

Finger Clicking Reads by Shoo Rayner

❏ Rock-a-doodle-do!   1 84121 465 5
❏ Treacle, Treacle, Little Tart   1 84121 469 8

Grandpa Turkey's Tall Tales by Jonathan Allen

❏ King of the Birds   1 84121 877 4
❏ And Pigs Might Fly   1 84121 710 7

The One and Only by Laurence Anholt and Tony Ross

❏ Micky the Muckiest Boy   1 86039 983 5
❏ Ruby the Rudest Girl   1 86039 623 2
❏ Harold the Hairiest Man   1 86039 624 0

And many more!